This Little Tiger book
belongs to:

_____

_____

_____

For Mark, for your endless love and support ~ TC

For Jacob ~ TW

LITTLE TIGER PRESS
1 The Coda Centre,
189 Munster Road, London SW6 6AW
www.littletiger.co.uk

First published in Great Britain 2015
This edition published 2015
Text copyright © Tracey Corderoy 2015
Illustrations copyright © Tim Warnes 2015
Visit Tim Warnes at www.ChapmanandWarnes.com
Tracey Corderoy and Tim Warnes have asserted their rights
to be identified as the author and illustrator of this work
under the Copyright, Designs and Patents Act, 1988
A CIP catalogue record for this book is available from the British Library
All rights reserved

ISBN 978-1-84869-134-6
LTP/1400/1133/0315
Printed in China
2 4 6 8 10 9 7 5 3 1

MORE!

Tracey Corderoy

Tim Warnes

LITTLE TIGER PRESS
London

Archie was a very
BUSY rhino.

His space-station model was bigger
than Mum. And bigger than Dad.
But still NOT big ENOUGH!

Archie was a very HUNGRY rhino too.

Would you like a cake, Archie?

Ooo – yes, please, Granny!

I'll just have one more . . .

And two more . . .

Yum-yum! **MORE!**

And Archie was a very NOISY rhino.

But even at quiet times, he ALWAYS
wanted more . . .

Whatever Archie liked,
he liked it
a LOT.

And whatever Archie did, he always did that *little* bit extra . . .

Archie's costume was
AMAZING. Everyone
thought so . . .

But it did make Archie too **slow**
to catch up . . .

too **heavy** to bounce . . .

Maybe "more" WASN'T
always more fun.

Maybe "more" was sometimes
TOO MUCH . . .

wheeeee!

Except, of course . . .

. . . when it came to having more

FRIENDS!